MR
LITTLE MISS
go Outside

Roger Hargreaves

Hello, my name is Walter. Can you spot me in this book?

Original concept by
Roger Hargreaves

Written and illustrated by

Mr Busy had been cooped up inside all winter long and now the weather had cheered up he could not wait to get outside.

He headed out into the great outdoors with a long list of things he wanted to do.

The first thing on his list was to build a treehouse.

Now, there are all sorts of treehouses.

There were simple ones like Little Miss Quick's.

Who was in too much of a rush to finish it properly!

There were extravagant ones like Little Miss Splendid's.

And there were extraordinary ones like
Mr Impossible's.

A treehouse without a tree!

Being the busy fellow Mr Busy was, he had built his treehouse in no time at all.

Most people would have wanted to enjoy their treehouse once they had finished it, but not Mr Busy.

He was looking for the next thing to do.

Busy old Mr Busy.

And the next thing was to build a dam.

Making dams is great fun, sloshing around getting wet and muddy before you break it all apart.

Mr Busy built a splendid dam, but did he wait around for it to fill up and go for a swim?

Of course not!

Mr Busy was off and running to his next outdoor activity.

Flying a kite!

Mr Busy loved all the running around and getting the kite in the air bit, but he wasn't so keen on the standing still and flying it bit, so he gave his kite to someone else …

Mr Small!

It was lucky Mr Tall was there to stop Mr Small flying away!

To make the most of the fine weather, Mr Busy wanted to fit as many things into his day as possible.

He consulted his list.

Riding a bike.

Playing tennis.

Going on a bug hunt.

Easy peasy.

Mr Busy could do all of these at once!

And then it was time for lunch.

It had to be a picnic.

Little Miss Sunshine brought the rug.

Mr Fussy brought the sandwiches.

Little Miss Lucky brought the good weather.

And Mr Nonsense brought …

A lamp!

To fill the rest of his afternoon, Mr Busy went to his favourite place in the world.

A treetops adventure park.

There was lots to keep him busy there.

He zipped down the zip wire with Little Miss Brave.

He swung on the monkey ropes with Mr Tickle.

Not that Mr Tickle needed the ropes!

Watch out Mr Tickle - Mr Busy is coming!

Mr Busy bounced across the treetop crossing with Mr Bounce.

Be careful Little Miss Whoops!

And Mr Busy scrambled up the rope net with Little Miss Somersault.

Thank goodness the net was there!

After his long busy day outside, you would have imagined that Mr Busy would have been glad to go inside and relax in front of the telly.

But you would have imagined wrong.

It takes a lot more than that to tire out Mr Busy.

So, what do you think he did do when he got home?

He built another treehouse!